CHEECH
THE SCHOOL BUS DRIVER

by Cheech Marin
illustrated by Orlando L. Ramírez

HarperCollinsPublishers

GOOD MORNING!

My name is Cheech, and I'll be your school bus driver today. I am a really, really, really, REALLY good bus driver. I always get to school on time, and I never, ever, ever, EVER get lost.

The kids on my bus usually carry backpacks and schoolbooks. But one Monday, the kids got on the bus with musical instruments instead.

"I'm not falling for that old trick," I told them.

"What old trick?" Dolores asked.

"You're planning to sneak up behind me and blow that saxophone right in my ear, aren't you? That's not funny! Not at all!"

"We wouldn't do that to you," Oscar said. "You're our favorite bus driver."

Carmen laughed. "We're just starting a mariachi band, to play in the Battle of the Bands! And we named ourselves the Cheecharrones!"

"Battle of the Bands?" I said. "That reminds me of when I was a kid. I had a band with my friends too. Playing in a band was crazy and wild and groovanova!"

"Groovanova's not a real word, Cheech," Dolores said.

"It might not be a real word," I said. "But it's a real dance!"

Weeks went by. The kids practiced and practiced and practiced and practiced. And then they practiced even more. They shined their shoes and their instruments. They even washed all the dishes. Of course, that wasn't for the band. That was just doing their chores.

Finally the big day arrived. The Cheecharrones put on their matching outfits and hats. And they even combed their hair. They were ready. And they sounded great. Groovanova!

I drove them to the club. But when they got off the bus, everyone pointed and laughed. "Mariachi?" they said. "Battle of the Bands is for rock and roll!"

That made the Cheecharrones nervous, so I said, "Mariachi can beat rock and roll any day!"

But I was nervous too.

Inside the club, a band was already onstage. The band was called the Monsters. And they sounded like monsters. The band was so loud that we had to cover our ears!

But the audience was even louder than the band. The whole crowd was talking, and yelling everything they said. The band was loud, but nobody was listening.

"If the crowd talks this loudly while we play, no one will be able to hear us at all!" Claudia said. "We're too quiet! We'll get last place!"

The kids began to panic. "Quick!" Eugene said. "Let's borrow some drums and amps and go practice in the parking lot!"

"I don't like this idea," I said. But no one ever listens to Cheech.

Serena shouted, "With drums and amps, we'll be loud enough to win!"

But it was too LOUD!

The next band was called the Silver Snakes. They wore funny clothes. They looked kind of like Christmas trees. Or maybe dogs that just rolled in the garbage. They reminded me of those kids who don't know what to be for Halloween so they just put on *everything!*

Oscar got excited about their clothes. "Wait a minute!" Oscar said. "It's not how loud you are that makes you a good band. It's how cool you look!"

But the costumes didn't look **COOL** at all.

The last band was called The Humongous Spiders. The singer dressed like a spider, and the rest of the band dressed like flies. During the song, the singer pretended to eat the rest of the band!

"What a crazy show!" I said.

"That's it! Just what we need! A crazy show," Joey said.

"I don't know about that," I told him.

"No, Cheech. Joey is right," Carmen said. "We need something that will get everyone's attention, something spectacular."

But it wasn't
SPECTACULAR.

Then a man came outside.

"It's your turn, guys," he said. "You're on."

"Oh no!" I shouted. "We're out of time!"

We got up onstage. Everyone was watching us. I was really, really, really, REALLY nervous. Then something cool happened!

The Cheecharrones started playing just the way they had practiced—not too loud, not too soft, with lots of rhythm and style.

And everybody noticed how much quieter it was all of a sudden. The audience stopped talking so they could hear the music. Everyone leaned in close to the stage.

And that's how mariachi beat rock and roll!

To my children—Carmen, Joey, and Jasmine.

—C.M.

My special thanks to my loving family, who just never stopped
giving themselves in countless ways. To my wife, Ewa, for your
great support. And to Pamela, for always believing in yourself.

—O.L.R.

Cheech the School Bus Driver
Text copyright © 2007 by Cheech Marin
Illustrations copyright © 2007 by Orlando L. Ramirez

Library of Congress Cataloging-in-Publication Data is available.
ISBN-10: 0-06-113201-2 (trade bdg.) — ISBN-13: 978-0-06-113201-8 (trade bdg.)
ISBN-10: 0-06-113202-0 (lib. bdg.) — ISBN-13: 978-0-06-113202-5 (lib. bdg.)

Designed by Stephanie Bart-Horvath
1 2 3 4 5 6 7 8 9 10
❖
First Edition